Baffin Bay
Kangiqtugaapik
(Clyde River)
Davis Strait
Qikiqtarjuaq
(Broughton Island)
AUYUITTUQ
NATIONAL PARK
Pangniqtuuq
Pangnirtung
Cumberland Sound
Iqaluit
Kinngait
(Cape Dorset)
Kimmirut
(Lake Harbour)
Frobisher Bay
Hudson Strait
Quebec
Baffin Island
CANADA
UNITED STATES
MEXICO

ᐅᕿᑦᑐᕐᒧᑦ, ᐃᑭᓪᓗᐊᖅ, ᐊᐃᓴ ᐊᒻᒪᓗ ᐊᑭᕈᖅ, ᐊᓈᓇᑦᓯᐊᕐᓄᓪᓗ

For Ohito, Ekidlua, Isa and Akiruk,
and my grandmother

ᓇᐃᓇ ᒫᓂᖕ-ᑐᑉᓄ ᐃᓄᑦᑎᑑᓕᐊᖕᒋᑦ

Translated by Nina Manning-Toonoo

ᐃᓕᑕᕆᔭᐅᔪᑦ

ᐃᓕᑕᕆᔪᒪᔭᒃᑲ ᐃᑲᔪᖅᓯᓂᕆᓯᒪᔭᖕᒋᑦ ᖅᑭᓄᐃᓵᕐᓂᕆᓯᒪᔭᖕᒋᓪᓗ ᑎᐅᕆ ᕋᐃᐊᓐ-ᑯᒃ ᓕᐊᔅᓕ ᕗᐃᑦ ᕋᐃᐊᓐ-ᑯᒃ, ᑭᓐᖓᐃᑦ ᑯᐊᐸᒃᑯᖕᒋᓐᓂ ᐊᒻᒪᓗ ᐊᐃᑉᐸᕋ, ᓯᒥᐅᓂ. ᕐᖁᔭᓐᓇᒦᕈᒪᒻᒥᔭᕋ ᖅᑭᒥᕐᕈᐊᓚᑕᐅᖅᑎ ᑕᒪᑦᓱᒥᖓ ᑲᔪᓯᑦᑎᓯᓂᖓᓄᑦ.

ACKNOWLEDGMENTS

I would like to acknowledge the support and patience of Terry Ryan and Leslie Boyd Ryan, the West Baffin Co-op and my spouse, Simionie. I would also like to thank the publisher for making this into a reality.

Fourth printing 2018

Groundwood Books / House of Anansi Press
groundwoodbooks.com

We gratefully acknowledge for their financial support of our publishing program the Canada Council for the Arts, the Ontario Arts Council and the Government of Canada.

Canada Council for the Arts
Conseil des Arts du Canada

With the participation of the Government of Canada
Avec la participation du gouvernement du Canada | Canada

Library and Archives Canada Cataloguing in Publication

Teevee, Ningeokuluk
Alego / Ningeokuluk Teevee.

Text in Inuktitut and English
ISBN 978-0-88899-943-6

1. Inuit–Juvenile fiction. 2. Marine animals–Juvenile fiction
I. Title.

PS8639.E35A64 2009 jC813'.6 C2009-900288-4

The illustrations are in graphite and colored pencil on paper.
Designed by Michael Solomon
Printed and bound in Malaysia

ᐊᓕᒍᖅ
Alego

ᐅᓂᒃᑳᖓ ᑎᑎᖅᑐᒐᖏᓪᓗ

STORY AND PICTURES BY

ᓂᖏᐅᑯᓗᒃ ᑏᕕ

Ningeokuluk Teevee

GROUNDWOOD BOOKS
HOUSE OF ANANSI PRESS
TORONTO BERKELEY

ᖃᐅᑕᒫᒐᓚᒃ, ᐊᓕᒍᖅ ᑕᑯᓂᐊᖅᐸᑦᑐᒥᓂᖅ ᐊᓈᓇᑦᓯᐊᒥᓂᒃ, ᐊᓈᓇᑦᓯᐊᖅ. ᐅᓪᓗᒥ ᓂᕆᐅᓇᐃᑦᑐᖃᖅᐳᖅ.

"ᑎᓂᓕᖅᒪᑦ, ᐊᒻᒨᒪᔾᔭᐊᓚᖕᒐᒐᑦᑕ," ᐅᖃᖅᑐᖅ ᐊᓈᓇᑦᓯᐊᖅ.

ᐊᓕᒍᖅ ᐊᒻᒨᒪᔾᔭᐊᓚᐅᖅᓯᒪᓐᖏᓐᓇᒥ ᖁᕕᐊᓗᐊᓕᖅᑐᖅ.

Most days Alego would go to see her grandmother – Anaaanatsiaq. Today there was a surprise.

"It's almost low tide, and we are going clam digging," said Anaaanatsiaq.

Alego had never gone clam digging before and she was excited.

ᐊᓕᒍᖅ ᐊᐱᕆᔪᖅ ᐊᓈᓇᑦᓯᐊᒥᓂᒃ ᓇᒦᒪᖔᑕ ᐊᒻᒨᒪᔪᐃᑦ ᖃᓄᕐᓗ ᐱᔭᐅᓲᖑᒻᒪᖔᑕ.

"ᐊᒻᒨᒪᔪᐃᑦ ᓯᐅᕐᕿᒥᐅᑕᐃᑦ. ᑕᑯᒍᕕᑦ ᑭᓐᓇᕐᓂᒃ ᓯᐅᕐᕿᒥ, ᑕᐃᒪ ᐊᒻᒨᒪᔪᖅᑕᖅᑯᖅ. ᓴᒡᒐᕐᓗᒍ ᑭᓐᓇᐅᑉ ᐊᕙᑖᒍᑦ ᐊᒻᒨᒪᔪᖅᓯᓇᖓᔪᑎᑦ. ᐃᓛᓐᓂᒃᑯᓪᓗ ᑕᑯᖃᑦᑕᓇᖓᔪᑎᑦ ᐅᓯᖓ ᐊᓃᖅᑎᓪᓗᒍ ᓯᐅᕐᕿᐅᑉ ᖄᖓᓂ. ᑎᒍᓵᕐᓗᒍ ᐊᒧᑦᑕᖅᑲᐃᑦ."

Alego asked Anaanatsiaq where the clams were and how to catch them.

"Ammuumajuit live in the sand. If you see holes in the sand, that's where the clams are. Dig around a hole and you will find a clam. Sometimes you will see the foot of the clam above the sand. Then you grab it and pull it out."

ᑎᑭᐅᑎᒐᒥᒃ ᓯᓈᓄᑦ, ᐊᓕᒍᖅ ᕿᕕᐊᕋᓕᖅᑐᒥᓂᖅ ᑕᑯᑦᓯᓂᓗ ᐃᒧᓪᓗᐊᓗᓐᓂᒃ ᐱᑭᐊᖕᒐᔪᓂᒃ ᓯᐅᕋᒥ. ᐊᑦᑐᐃᑕᖅᑯᖅ ᓴᒡᒐᐅᑎᒥᓄᑦ ᐊᐅᓚᔾᔭᑦᓯᓂ ᑎᒻᒥᑲᑦᑕᖅᑯᖅ ᑮᓇᓪᓗᐊᖕᒐᓄᕐ!

When they reached the seashore Alego looked around and saw a couple of wrinkly things sticking out of the sand. She poked one with her trowel, and it moved and squirted her right in the face!

ᐱᓱᒃᑲᒥᒃ ᑖᕗᖕᒐᒥᐊᖅ ᓯᓈᒃᑯᑦ, ᐊᓚᒍᖅ ᑕᑯᑦᑕᖅᑯᖅ ᐊᐅᓚᔾᔪᑦᑐᒥᒃ ᐃᖂᑎᓂ. ᑕᑯᒥᐊᑦᓴᓯᐊᕆᒥᐅᒃ ᑕᑯᑦᓴᐅᑎᒋᓐᖏᑦᑐᖅ. ᐃᖂᑏᑦ ᐊᐅᓚᔾᔭᓚᕐᒥᒻᒪᑕ ᑕᑯᓚᖅᓱᒍᓗ - ᑲᓇᔪᖅ ᓅᑦᓱᓇᐃᓪᓚᔪᖅ ᑎᓄᔾᔭᐅᓯᒪᒐᒥ.

As they walked farther along the shore Alego saw something moving in the seaweed. She went to take a closer look, but at first she couldn't see anything. Then the seaweed moved again, and there it was – a sculpin trapped on the shore because the tide had gone out.

ᑲᓇᔪᐃᑦ ᐊᖏᔪᐊᓗᓐᓂᒃ ᑲᐱᓐᓇᖅᑐᓕᓐᓂᒃ ᓂᐊᕐᑯᖃᕐᒪᑕ ᐃᓵᖓᔫᖅᓯᑎᓪᓗ ᐊᖒᑎᖏᑦ, ᑕᖅᓴᖏᓪᓗ ᑕᑯᔭᕐᓃᑦᑐᐸᓘᑦᓯᑎᒃ.

Kanajuit have big spiny heads and fan-like fins, and their camouflage makes them very hard to spot.

ᑖᕙᓂᒋᐊᒃᑲᓐᓂᒐᑖᑐᐃᓐᓇᖅ ᐊᓕᒍᖅ ᑎᑭᐅᑎᓕᖓᕗᖅ
ᐃᒃᑲᑦᑐᕈᓗᒻᒧᑦ ᑕᓯᐊᕿᕈᖅᓯᒪᔪᒧᑦ. ᑕᑯᑦᓱᓂᓗ ᐃᒫᓃᑦᑐᒥᒃ.
ᐊᐅᐸᔮᖕᒐᔪᐹᓗᒃ ᐊᒡᒐᐅᔭᖅ ᐅᔭᕋᐅᑉ ᖄᖕᒐᓃᑦᑐᖅ!

Just a little farther along Alego came upon a shallow pool of water. Something inside caught her eye. It was a bright orange starfish sitting on a rock!

ᐊᓕᒍᖅ ᑕᑯᓕᖅᑐᖅ ᖃᓄᐃᑦᑐᑐᐃᓐᓇᑦᓯᐊᓂᒃ ᐆᒪᔪᓂᒃ ᐃᒪᕐᒥ - ᐱᓱᐊᖅᔪᑦᑐᐊᓗᒻᒥᒃ ᖁᐱᕐᕈᐊᓗᒻᒥᒃ ᓂᐅᕋᓴᖃᖅᓱᓂ ᑕᐃᔭᐅᔪᖅ ᐅᒡᔪᓐᓇᖅ ᐊᒻᒪᓗ ᓯᐅᐱᕈᐃᑦ ᖃᓄᐃᑦᑐᑐᐃᓐᓇᐃᑦ ᓴᓇᒻᒪᖕᒋᑦ ᐊᖕᒋᓂᖕᒋᓪᓗ, ᐃᓚᖕᒐᑦ ᐊᓪᓛᑦ ᑎᑦᑐᓚᐅᖅᑎᖅᔫᔮᖅᓱᓂ, ᑕᐃᔭᐅᔪᖅ ᓯᐅᐱᕈᖅ. ᑭᖑᕋᓵᓗᐃᓪᓗ. ᑭᖑ ᒥᑭᔪᕈᓗᒃ ᐃᒪᕐᒥᐅᑕᖅ ᖁᐱᕐᕈᖅ ᓯᓚᑉᐱᐊᖃᖅᓱᓂ ᐊᒥᓱᐊᓗᓐᓂᓪᓗ ᓂᐅᖃᖅᓱᓂ. ᐅᓪᓗᕆᐊᖅᔫᔮᖅᑐᓪᓕ ᑕᐃᔭᐅᔪᖅ ᐊᒡᒐᐅᔭᖅ, ᐊᒡᒐᖅᔫᔮᕐᒪᑦ.

"ᐅᑎᕆᐊᖃᓕᕐᑕ", ᐊᓈᓇᑦᓯᐊᖅ ᐅᖃᖅᑐᖅ. "ᖃᐃᒋᑦ ᑕᑯᓚᒃᑲ ᐊᒻᒨᒪᔪᖅᑕᑎᑦ." ᐊᓕᒍᖅ ᑕᑯᑦᓱᓂ ᐊᓈᓇᑦᓯᐊᖕᒐᑕ ᖃᑦᑕᖕᒐᓂᒃ ᑕᑕᑦᑐᒥᒃ ᐊᒻᒨᒪᔪᕐᓂᒃ.

Alego saw that there were all kinds of living things in the water – a creepy-crawly thing with many legs called ugjunnaq and shells in different shapes and sizes, even one shaped like a horn called siupiruq. There were lots of kinguit, too. The kinguq is a tiny sea creature with a protective shell and many small legs. The starfish is called aggaujaq, because it looks like a hand.

"It's time to go back," called Anaaanatsiaq. "Come here and show me your catch."

Alego could see that Anaaanatsiaq's pot was full of ammuumajuit.

"ᖃᐃᒥᑦ, ᐊᓈᓇᑦᓯᐊᒃ. ᑕᑯᓗᓂᖅ!"

"Here, Anaanatsiaq. Look!"

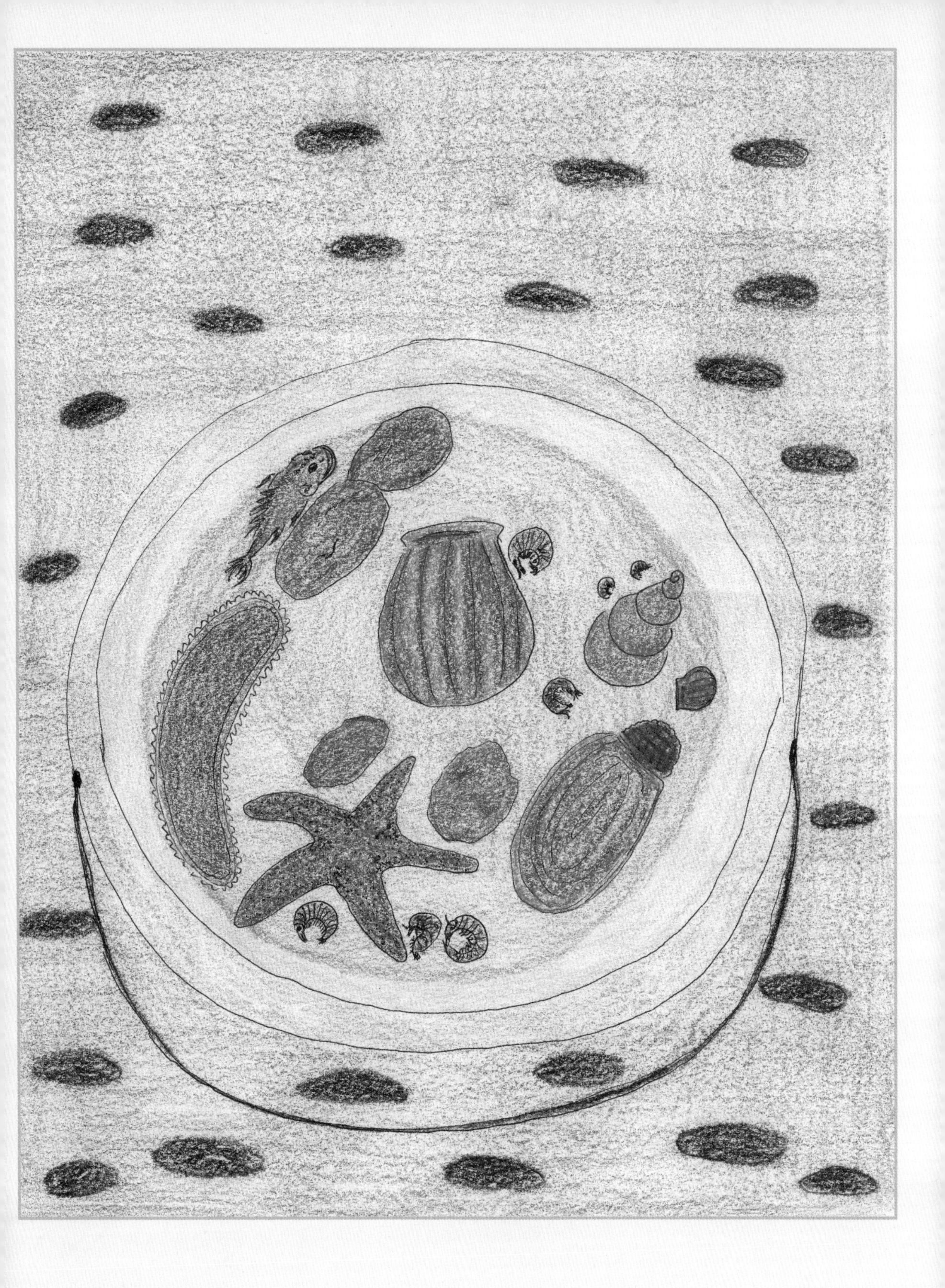

ᐋᓈᓇᑦᓯᐊᖅ ᐃᔪᓯᑦᑕᖅᑯᖅ.

"ᐋᑏ," ᖃᐃᕐᑯᔨᑦᑕᖅᑯᖅ ᐋᓈᓇᑦᓯᐊᖅ. "ᐊᖏᕐᕿᓚᖅᑕ ᐅᓚᓐᖏᓐᓂᖕᒐᓂ ᐅᓗᔾᔭᐅᖏᓐᓂᑎᓐᓂ."

Anaanatsiaq chuckled.

"Atii," she called. "Let's go home before the tide comes back in and the shore is covered with water again."

ᐊᖏᕐᕋᕋᒥᒃ, ᐊᓕᒎᖅ ᐊᓈᓇᑦᓯᐊᖓᓗ ᑲᔾᔫᖅᑐᐹᓘᑦᓯᑎᒃ ᐊᒻᒨᒪᔪᖅᑐᖃᑎᖃᓕᖅᑑᒃ ᐆᓇᖅᑐᒥᓪᓗ ᑏᑐᖃᑎᖃᖅᓯᑎᒃ ᐋᑕᑦᓯᐊᒥᒃ, ᐋᑕᑦᓯᐊᖅ, ᐅᖅᑰᓯᒋᐊᕈᑎᒋᑦᓯᒋᑦ ᐱᓯᑯᑖᓚᐅᖅᓯᑎᒃ ᐊᑦᓯᕉᓚᐅᖅᓯᑎᓪᓗ.

"ᒪᒪᖅᑐᖅ!" ᐊᓕᒎᖅ ᐅᖃᓕᖅᑐᖅ, ᐊᖏᖃᑎᒌᑦᑐᐃᓐᓇᓕᖅᓯᑎᓪᓗ. ᒪᒪᖅᑐᖅ!

When they got home Alego and Anaanatsiaq enjoyed a feast of clams and hot tea with Grandfather – Ataatatsiaq – to warm them up after their long walk and hard work.

"Mamaqtuq!" Alego said, and they all agreed. Delicious!

FLOUR
SUGAR
TEA

ᑐᑭᓯᒋᐊᕈᑏᑦ

GLOSSARY

ᐊᒻᒨᒪᔪᖅ/ᐊᒻᒨᒪᔪᐃᑦ
ammuumajuq / ammuumajuit

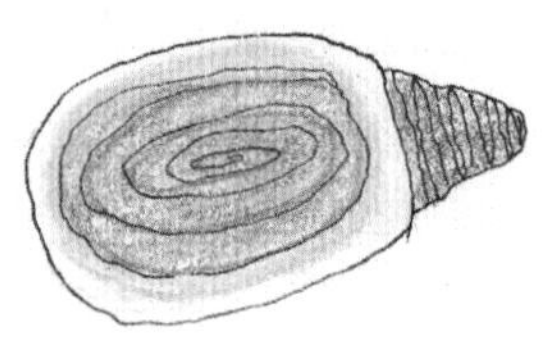

clam / clams

ᑲᓇᔪᖅ/ᑲᓇᔪᐃᑦ
kanajuq / kanajuit

sculpin / sculpins

ᐊᒡᒐᐅᔭᖅ
aggaujaq

starfish

ᐅᒡᔪᓐᓇᖅ - ᕐᑯᐱᕐᕈᖅ ᓂᐅᕋᓴᓚᒃ
ugjunnaq

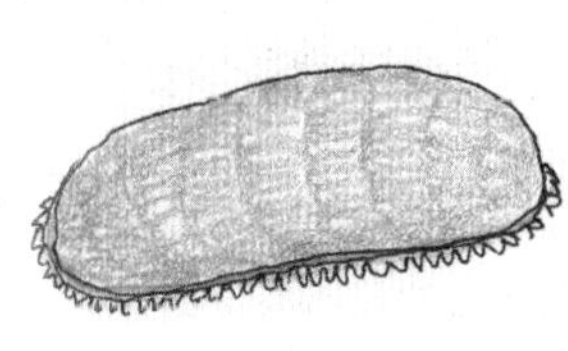

creepy-crawly thing with many legs

ᓯᐅᐱᕈᖅ
siupiruq

snail

ᑭᖑᒃ/ᑭᖑᐃᑦ
kinguq / kinguit

sea louse / sea lice

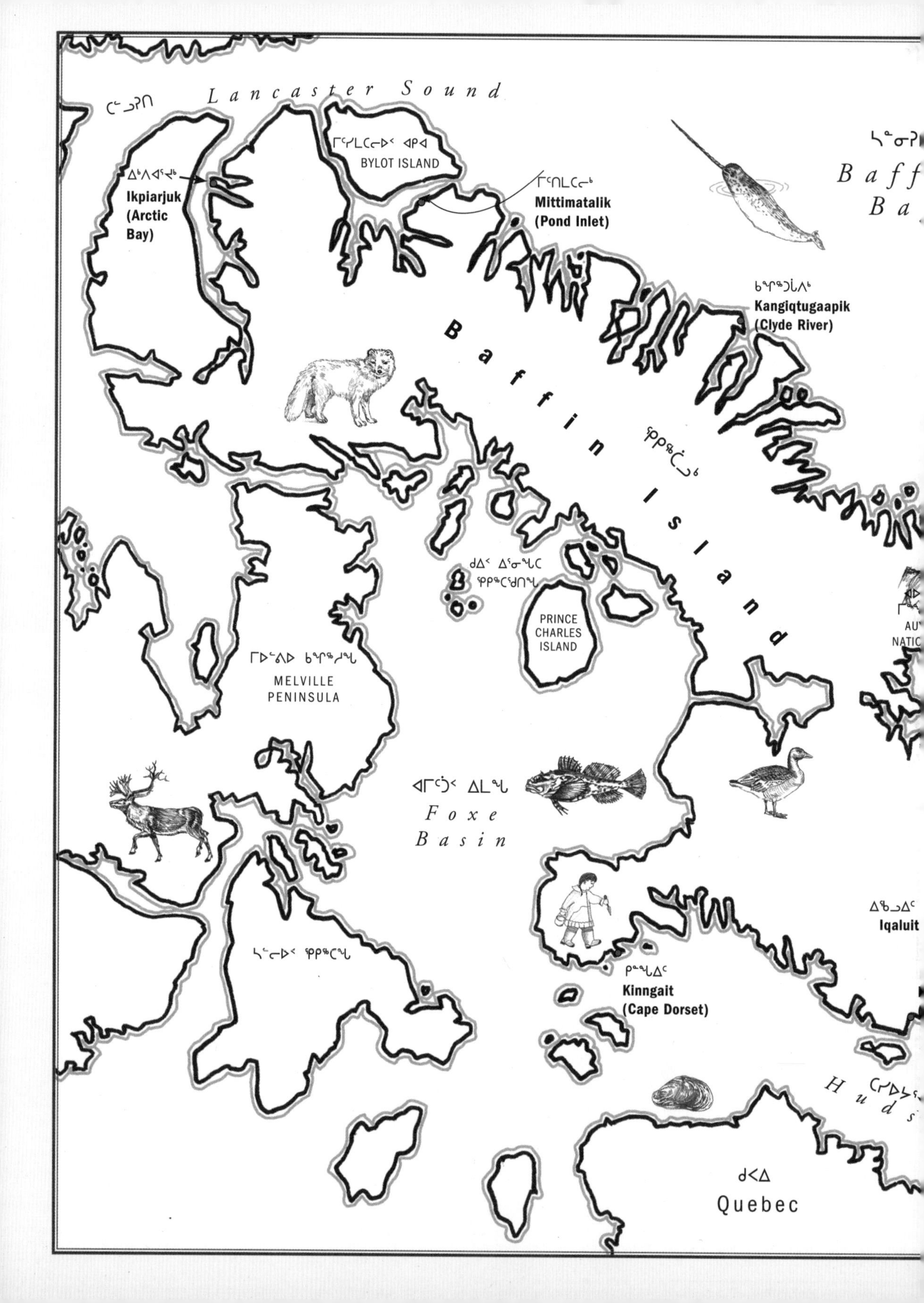

Lancaster Sound
ᐃᒃᐱᐊᕐᔪᒃ
Ikpiarjuk (Arctic Bay)
BYLOT ISLAND
ᒥᑦᑎᒪᑕᓕᒃ
Mittimatalik (Pond Inlet)
ᑲᖏᖅᑐᒑᐱᒃ
Kangiqtugaapik (Clyde River)
Baffin Island
PRINCE CHARLES ISLAND
MELVILLE PENINSULA
Foxe Basin
ᐃᖃᓗᐃᑦ
Iqaluit
ᑭᙵᐃᑦ
Kinngait (Cape Dorset)
ᑯᐯᒃ
Quebec